DAVE and the FROG

Written by
Jenny Phillips

Illustrated by
Ekaterina Kolesnikova

Challenge Words

blue

Dave

good

saw

out

CHAPTER 1

Dave got up. He saw the sun in the sky.

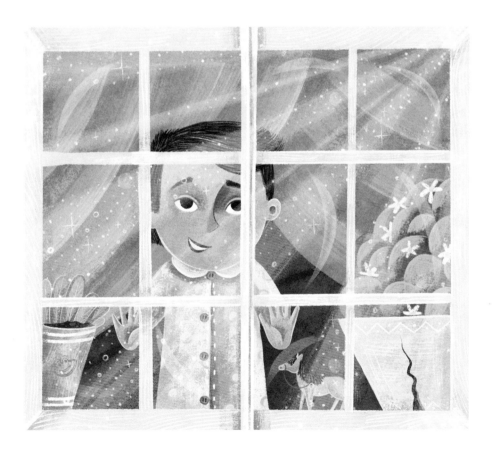

A bee buzzed by him.

It seemed to say, "Come! Come! Come and play!"

Dave got dressed. He had a glob of mush.

He helped Mom and Dad.

In the pen, he fed the pigs. Next, he got the eggs. Then he ran to Mom.

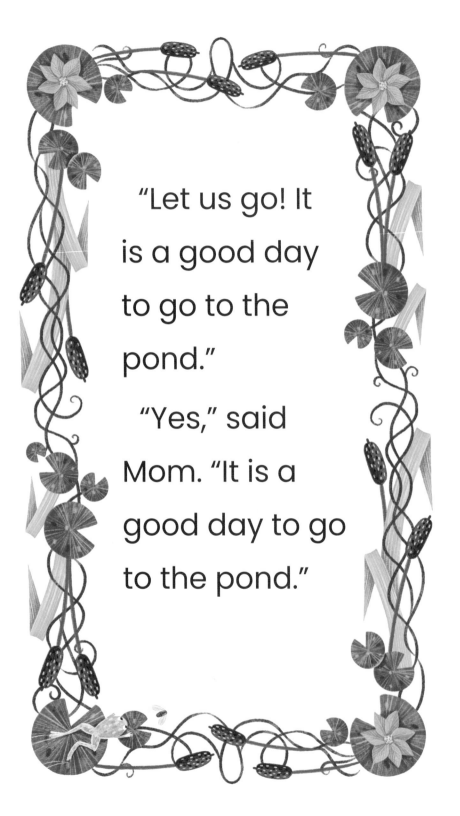

"Let us go! It is a good day to go to the pond."

"Yes," said Mom. "It is a good day to go to the pond."

She put good things in a
basket, and they left.

Up the hill they went. Into the trees they went. Out of the trees they went.

"There is the pond!"
yelled Dave. He ran to
the pond, still and flat as
glass.

"This is a good spot," said
Mom. "I will look at this,
and you can play."

Dave sat by the pond. He put his feet in, and a fish jumped.

Then he saw a green
thing by a big rock.

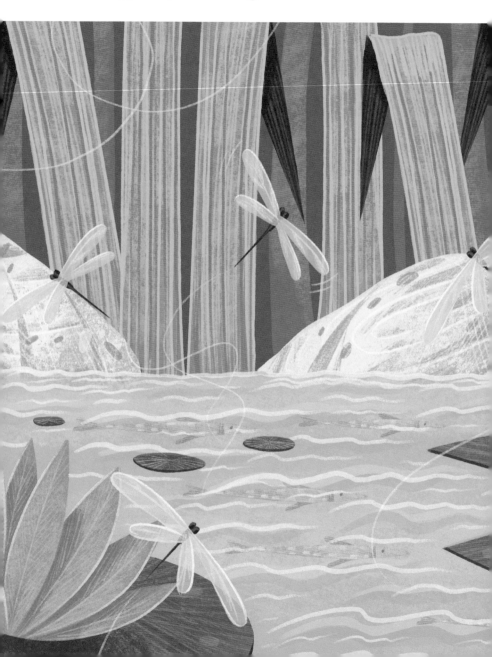

"A frog!" said Dave. "It can be my pet!"

Dave jumped at the frog.
The frog jumped in the
pond and swam fast. Dave
jumped in the pond and
swam fast.

"Dave!" said his mom. "You are all wet!"

"I have to get the frog, Mom!"

The frog hopped out of
the pond. Dave hopped
out of the pond.

Into the trees went the frog. Into the trees went Dave. Into the trees went Mom.

A log was in the way.
The frog jumped. Dave
jumped. Mom jumped.
The frog hid. Dave saw
him and picked him up.

"A pet! A pet for me," said Dave with glee.

"You must be good to it," said Mom.

"I will! I will!" said Dave.

CHAPTER 2

Dave filled his tub. He put some plants and things in it for the frog. The frog had a spot to sit.

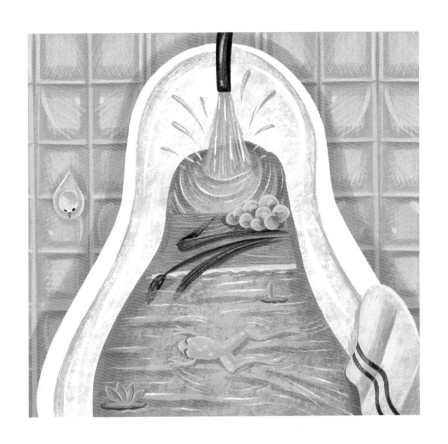

Dave called the frog
Ribbit.

All day, Ribbit swam in
the tub. He seemed glad
to be there.

"Mom, what is a good lunch for a frog?" asked Dave.

"Insects," said Mom.
Dave got a net. He went
out to get some insects.

It was a long time until he got a bug. He clapped his net.

He did
not get
a moth.

He did
not get a
cricket.

He did not
get a red
bug.

Yes! He
clapped
his net on
a fly.

Ribbit loved the fly, but it seemed like he needed a lot of insects.

"I will go get ten insects," said Dave.

It took a long, long, long time.

As Dave got in his bed, he said, "It is hard to have a pet, but I love Ribbit."

CHAPTER 3

The next day, Dave got up. He looked out his window. The fast wind bent the trees.

Dave went to check on Ribbit.

"OOOOooooohhhhhhh!"

Ribbit was not there! He was not in the tub.

"Ribbit is missing!" he said to Mom. Mom hugged Dave. "We will look for Ribbit."

They looked in this spot.

They looked in that spot.

Dad looked in a big chest.

Dave looked in a closet.

No Ribbit.

Dave was sad. He went
out and sat on a rock.

The sky was not blue.

Dave felt a little blue.

Just then, Dave saw a

green thing hopping on
the path.

"Ribbit!"

The frog was going to the pond.

Ribbit hopped. Dave

hopped and hopped.
Mud splashed. Mom was
there, too.

Ribbit got to the pond.
Ribbit jumped in. Dave
wished to jump in.

"No!" said Mom, so Dave
stopped.

Dave saw Ribbit swim. He
saw Ribbit get a fly.

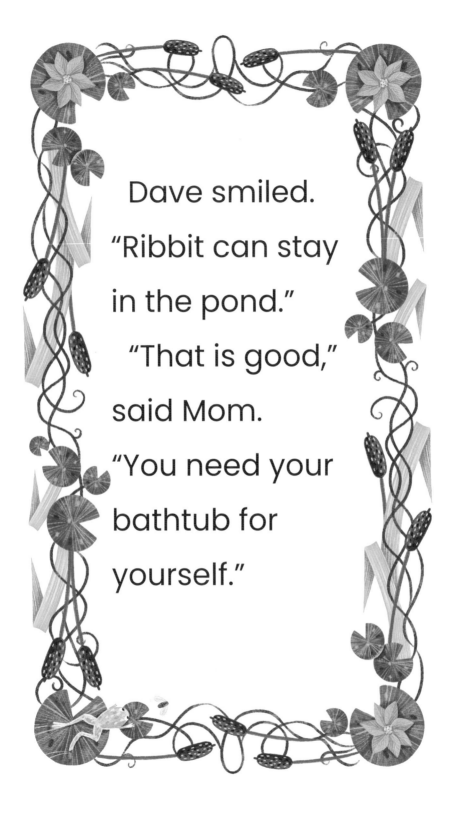

Dave smiled. "Ribbit can stay in the pond."

"That is good," said Mom. "You need your bathtub for yourself."

Dave looked at the mud on his skin.

"Yes, I do," said Dave. "Let us go."

Hand in hand, Dave and his mom went on the path.

"The best spot for Ribbit
is the pond," Dave said.

Check out these other Level 1B books from The Good and the Beautiful!

Jane and the King
By Jenny Phillips

Jack and the Lost Maze
By Jenny Phillips